Celia

Christelle Vallat

Illustrated by Stéphanie Augusseau

PETER PAUPER PRESS, INC.

White Plains, New York

First published in Belgium under the title *Zélie* by Christelle Vallat & Stéphanie Augusseau
Copyright © 2012 Alice Éditions
English translation copyright © 2014 Peter Pauper Press, Inc.
First published in the United States and United Kingdom in 2014 by Peter Pauper Press, Inc.

Published by Peter Pauper Press, Inc.
202 Mamaroneck Avenue
White Plains, New York 10601
U.S.A.

Published in the United Kingdom and Europe by Peter Pauper Press, Inc.
c/o White Pebble International
Unit 2, Plot 11 Terminus Rd.
Chichester, West Sussex PO19 8TX, UK

Library of Congress Cataloging-in-Publication Data

Vallat, Christelle, 1971-
    [Zelie. English]
    Celia / Christelle Vallat ; illustrated by Stephanie Augusseau. -- First English edition.
        pages cm
    "First published in Belgium under the title Zelie by Christelle Vallat & Stephanie Augusseau,
Copyright (c) 2012 Alice Editions."
    Summary: Celia, the town listener, collects a seed from each person who shares a problem with
her, so when Julian loses his seed on the way to see her, he is unable to let go of his sadness.
    ISBN 978-1-4413-1536-6 (hardcover : alk. paper) [1. Listening--Fiction. 2. Seeds--Fiction. 3.
Sadness--Fiction.] I. Augusseau, Stephanie, illustrator. II. Title.
    PZ7.V2538Cel 2014
    [E]--dc23
                                        2013040045

ISBN 978-1-4413-1536-6
Manufactured for Peter Pauper Press, Inc.
Printed in Hong Kong

7 6 5 4 3 2 1

Visit us at www.peterpauper.com

For Gabriel and Jules
C.V.

To all the Celias,
To all the open hearts,
To a group of wonderful friends.
S.A.

Every Sunday Celia would look out her window.
And every Sunday there they were.
A long line of many people, all in single file,
each patiently waiting their turn.

She would pick up her stool, sit down, and
motion for the first in line to come to her.

Each in turn, they would lean over and
begin to whisper in her ear.

And Celia listened.
She listened to the little problems, to the big problems.
She listened to all the in-between problems.
She listened to every worry, every sorrow,
everything that the people had to say.

And when they let go of their worries,
they would feel lighter and happier.

In exchange for Celia's kind service,
they would each give her a seed.

One Sunday a little boy named Julian stood in line.
He was feeling blue and wanted Celia's help.

But when he reached in his back pocket to get his seed,
it wasn't there! Oh no! He quietly stepped away from the line.
He would have to hold on to his sadness.

At the end of the day, Celia gathered up all of the seeds and put them in her wheelbarrow.

Tomorrow she would begin her journey.

Monday began like every other Monday did for Celia.
She walked into the town square, chose a few seeds from
her wheelbarrow, and gently blew on them . . .

. . . and *poof!* They became beautiful balloons!

Celia walked by the baker's shop
and threw some seeds into the
open windows . . .

. . . and *presto!* They frosted all of the cupcakes and cookies!

Celia traveled to the countryside.
She tossed some seeds up into the air.
They floated gently, landing on a tree,
decorating it with apples!

As Celia continued along the bumpy road,
she saw something in the dirt.

"What is that I see?" she asked herself.
"Why, it's a seed."

She picked it up and peered closely at it.
"Oh dear," she said. "This seed belongs to an unhappy child."

She slipped the seed into her pocket and continued on her way.

At the top of the hill the gardener was waiting for her.
"Hello, Celia! What will it be today? Tulips? Petunias?"

Celia carefully gathered a handful of seeds, and sowed
them into the four winds . . .

. . . and *presto!* The hill was filled with blooming flowers.

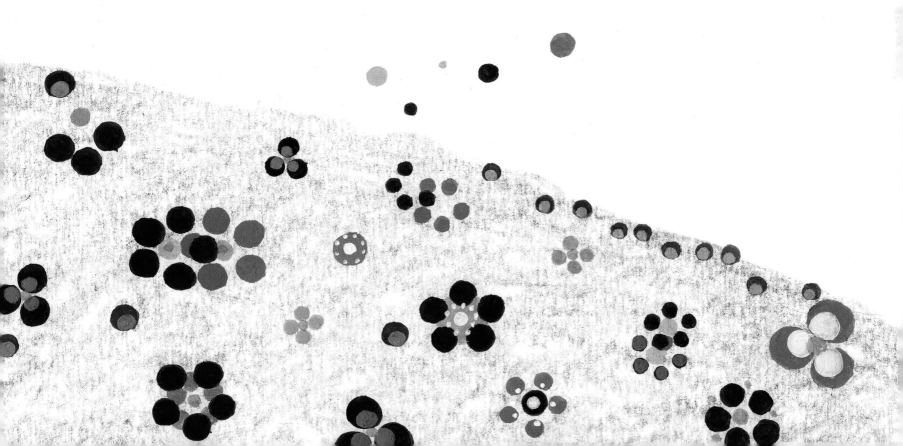

It was getting late and the moon rose in the darkening sky. Celia climbed a large ladder with a handful of seeds. As she hung the seeds, one by one, they turned into stars, sparkling in the night.

"Ah, that's much better," she said.

Another day was done and it was time to return home.

On her way back, Celia saw Julian sitting on the side of the road.

Julian sighed.

"What's wrong, my child?" Celia asked.

"I lost my seed yesterday and couldn't see you," said Julian. "I couldn't let go of my sadness."

"Look," said Celia, as she pulled the
seed out of her pocket.

Julian's eyes lit up. It was his seed!

"Is it too late?" asked Julian.

"No, no. Come with me," replied Celia.
"I will show you."

Julian followed Celia to her little cottage.

Celia brought out a flower pot, and they planted the seed in the dirt. Julian sprinkled the seed with water.

And then he waited.

Julian visited the seed every day.

He wanted to see it grow.

Sometimes Julian and Celia would talk.

And sometimes Celia would offer Julian a cookie.

And time passed by . . .

Until one day, a tiny flower,
no larger than the tip of his nose,
appeared.

Julian came running. He was so excited!

He gave Celia a big hug.

His heart felt lighter,

and his world was filled . . .

. . . with happiness.